A Lucky Author Has A Dog

Written by **Mary Lyn Ray**   Illustrated by **Steven Henry**

Arthur A. Levine Books   An Imprint of Scholastic Inc.

LIBRARY OF CONGRESS CATALOGING-IN-PUBLICATION DATA

Ray, Mary Lyn, author. A lucky author has a dog / written by Mary Lyn Ray ;
illustrated by Steven Henry.   pages   cm
Summary: It is a lucky author who has a dog to greet her in the morning
and help her with ideas, because everything is better with a dog—but a dog
who has an author is also lucky.
ISBN 978-0-545-51876-5 (hardcover : alk. paper) 1. Authors—Juvenile
fiction. 2. Dogs—Juvenile fiction. [1. Authors—Fiction.
2. Dogs—Fiction.] I. Henry, Steven, 1962– illustrator. II. Title.
PZ7.R210154Lu 2015   [E]—dc23   2014041966

10 9 8 7 6 5 4 3 2 1   15 16 17 18 19
Printed in China   38
First edition, September 2015

The art for this book was created using Corel Painter 12.
The final illustrations were based on original pencil sketches.
The text was set in Mrs. Eaves Bold. The display type was
set in Sprocket BT. Book design by Marijka Kostiw

RECYCLE

For all the dogs who,
of themselves, make us lucky
—MLR

Early in the morning, people are waking
and going to work.

So a dog is, too.

Because an author should also be waking.

A lucky author has a dog to begin every day
with a kiss—

then some help
getting dressed.

And a lucky dog has an author.

Because the author doesn't say good-bye and go out the door to go to work. The author just takes a piece of paper and begins to write—

and write
    and write.

The dog isn't exactly sure
what an author does.

But the dog can see
    it is important.

So the dog brings ideas.

A lucky author has a dog
                    who helps.

Some authors do go to an office.

Some stay in pajamas
and write in bed.

Some write in loud places,

some in quiet places.

Most authors
have favorite
writing places.

But, really,
an author can write
anywhere.

Sometimes an author has to write fast, if a story comes sudden and fast. Except most stories don't.

Authors often frown at blank paper.

Or they stare out the window.

Then a dog worries.

It looks as if the author is doing nothing.
But the author is at work, thinking.
Or maybe reaching for just the right word.
(The dog knows good words, like *ball*.
                    And *squirrel*.)

The dog is proud to have an author to help.

So the dog stays close by.

Every author needs
an encouraging friend—

and all day the dog is,

until the author can't
get anything right,
and the dog says,
Arruff! Enough!

A dog knows when
it's time for a walk.

But it's hard for an author
to stop being an author
and leave a story behind.

Yet there could be more, anywhere.

So the dog, always helpful, is sniffing for story
and the author is looking about—

until their noses bring them home.

Because their noses are remembering supper:
a red plate for the author, a red bowl for the dog.

A lucky dog has a red bowl
and an author.

In buildings and houses, now lights are turned off.
It is night: night that is dark for sleeping—

until a new idea nudges
the author awake. So one light
comes on. And the author sits up
and writes.

Soon the sun begins to color the sky, and people are again going to work. But today the author is already dressed before the dog wakes.

The dog knows something is different.

Quickly. Hurry. Come.
Then the door closes.
The dog is left
                at the window—

because it's Author Day at Fred C. Underhill School!

In every room, at every desk, is an author.
But one more has come as a guest.
So there are banners and questions:

"Do you like to write?"

"Doesn't your hand
get tired?"

"How do you get ideas?"

"Where do you get the words
to write with?"

"What do you do when you're stuck?"

A fan is waving both hands high.

"Can I have your autograph?"

Then EVERYONE asks.

"I'm giving these to my family
for Christmas," a fourth grader says.

At noon, lunch is orange and yellow.
The author isn't sure what it is.

But the author is brave and eats it.

Some of it.

After lunch there's time for book signing.

A first grader warns, "You shouldn't do *that.*
You'll get sent to the principal for writing in books."

A third grader asks, "Why do you always write
about dogs?"

Then, just as the bell is about to ring,
there's one last question everyone asks:
"WILL YOU WRITE ABOUT US?"

"I may," says the author.
"But why don't *you*
write about you?"

Someone has waited all day for the click of the door.

And now the author is home, smelling of school and its mysteries.

For a moment there's only author and dog.
    "Should we go for a walk?"

The author rubs two happy ears.
    A tail wags.
        A lucky dog has an author.

And a lucky author has a dog.

Are stories waiting to be noticed?
The dog will show the author how to look
and listen the way a dog does.

An author without a dog can learn.
But having a dog
                  is better.

Because everything
is better *with* a dog.